Chinese Children's Favorite Stories

Text and illustrations by
Mingmei Yip

TUTTLE PUBLISHING
Tokyo • Rutland, Vermont • Singapore

When my brother and I were very small, both our parents liked to read us bedtime stories. Sometimes, when Mother had tucked us in for the night, Father would come into the bedroom, wink at both of us, and then proudly say, "I'm the storyteller tonight."

I still remember how on many evenings, an arm around each of us, my young, handsome father would keep us spellbound with traditional Chinese tales—*The Monkey King, The Ghost Catcher, The Frog Who Lived in a Well*—either from memory or retold from the popular magazine, *Children's Happy Garden*. He would tell each story in a lively, animated manner, sometimes even jumping up to show us kung fu movements in imitation of the Monkey King or the Little Immortal. But Father's expression would become serious when he explained the story's moral—kindness and wisdom as in *The Wolf and the Scholar*, helping others as in *The Fish-Basket Goddess*, or overcoming obstacles as in the *Carp Jumping over the Dragon Gate*.

One night, after he had finished telling *The Frog Who Lived in a Well*, Father stared at us and asked, "You don't want to be like that frog, do you? Thinking that a tiny well is the whole universe, and he's the smartest fellow in the whole world?" He reached to pat our heads. "Remember, never be boastful, for there may always be a mountain higher than the one you live on."

I believe this is how children in China grow up and learn to meet life's challenges—by listening to tales filled with precious lessons passed down from their ancestors.

It is my hope that, by retelling some of these thousand-year-old Chinese stories, I can pass along the gift of my parents, their generous spirit and their love for children—and inspire other children for many generations to come.

—*Mingmei Yip*

Chinese Children's Favorite Stories

To my husband Geoffrey, for his compassion and wisdom
— Mingmei Yip

Published by Tuttle Publishing, an imprint of Periplus Editions
(HK) Ltd., with editorial offices at 364 Innovation Drive,
North Clarendon, VT 05759-9436 USA and 61 Tai Seng
Avenue, #02-12, Singapore 534167

LCC Card No. 2004101748
ISBN 978-0-8048-3589-3
Printed in Malaysia
First printing, 2004

12 11 10 09
10 9 8 7 6

Distributed by
North America, Latin America and Europe
Tuttle Publishing, 364 Innovation Drive,
North Clarendon, VT 05759-9436
Tel 1 (802) 773 8930, Fax 1 (802) 773 6993
Email: info@tuttlepublishing.com
Website: www.tuttlepublishing.com

Asia Pacific
Berkeley Books Pte Ltd, 61 Tai Seng Avenue,
#02-12, Singapore 534167
Tel (65) 6280 1330, Fax (65) 6280 6290
Email: inquiries@periplus.com.sg
Website: www.periplus.com

Japan
Tuttle Publishing, Yaekari Building, 3F 5-4-12,
Osaki, Shinagawa-ku, Tokyo, Japan 141-0032
Tel (81)3 5437 0171, Fax (81)3 5437 0755
Email: tuttle-sales@gol.com

Indonesia
PT Java Books Indonesia, Kawasan Industri Pulogadung,
Jl. Rawa Gelam IV No.9, Jakarta 13930, Indonesia
Tel (62) 21 4682 1088, Fax (62) 21 461 0206
Email: cs@javabooks.co.id

Contents

The Fish-Basket Goddess

Along time ago in ancient China, all roads to the capital of Luoyang were teeming every day with people from the four corners and five directions. Merchants came to trade silk and tea, and students arrived on the shore filled with hope for their luck in the imperial examinations. Parents bought sweet cakes and other goodies for their children to munch on while they watched puppets, acrobats, and lion dancers.

To reach the city gate, everyone had to cross a wide river. Crowds climbed onto boats where they would talk and laugh while watching the water sway like green silk. Sitting happily on the boat, they would open their shiny lacquer lunch boxes to enjoy picnics of pork buns, ginger chicken, steamed fish, and sweet tea.

One morning, the River Dragon King woke up in a terribly angry mood and, to spoil everyone else's day, began to stir up giant waves. As he thrashed his tail, all the boats capsized, spilling fathers, mothers, grandfathers, grandmothers, boys, girls, dogs, cats—and everybody else—into the raging river. Seeing them all flapping and flailing their limbs in the roaring water, he burst into laughter. "Ha! Ha! Look at that little boy soaking wet and struggling like a rat! And that round man bobbing like a watermelon! Oh, see that yellow dog, he can swim, but the wave took his bone away! And that angry cat, I bet she doesn't like getting wet! Ha! Ha! Ha!"

After that day, the dragon became very fond of this game of dunking people.

One little girl, after climbing onto the shore, began to cry. Her pork bun had sunk in the river and she had nothing to eat. Her poor, wet cat was howling miserably. Guan Yin, the Goddess of Compassion, heard the little girl and her cat and decided to come down to help.

The Goddess descended from her heavenly palace all the way to the river bank, where huge waves were splashing against the shore. She called out, "Dragon King! Dragon King! Please come! I have to talk to you!" The dragon had been having a sweet dream of eating a banquet of crab and shrimp when he was awakened by the Goddess's earnest calls. Annoyed, he quickly left his dragon bed and rose above the water. When he saw a beautiful young woman standing alone by the cliff, he was too surprised to say anything.

Guan Yin opened her mouth and said most respectfully, "Honorable Dragon King," she smiled, her face shining with compassion. "I'm here to ask you to stop making waves. They are certainly enjoyable to look at, but do you know that they have also made many people miserable?"

"Ha! Ha! Ha!" The Dragon King laughed until his whiskers shook. "Pretty lady, of course I know. That's what makes me happy!"

Guan Yin tried to be patient. "But many good people have suffered because of your happiness."

"Ha! Ha! Ha! Who cares! I'm having a lot of fun!" Not only did the Dragon King sneer at the Goddess's pleas, he decided to show off his power to this pretty woman. With a roar as loud as thunder, he thumped his tail as hard as he could, making waves leap up as high as mountains.

Seeing that the dragon would not be persuaded, Guan Yin flew back to heaven to think of something else. When she returned the next day, she transformed herself into a fishmonger and walked straight into the city's marketplace. At the busiest spot she set down her basket. Since she was very beautiful and the fish inside her basket were very fresh, with shiny scales and moving eyes, a crowd soon started to gather around her.

Everyone wanted to see the beautiful fishmonger and in a few minutes all the fish were sold. Still, the people crowded around her. With her bright eyes smiling, she said, "Dear ladies and gentlemen, since I have no more fish to sell, we can play a game." She paused and then said, "The one who can toss the most money into my basket shall become my husband. But the money that misses the basket will be used to build a bridge so that you can all walk safely over the Dragon King's river."

The crowd cheered.

A young man cast the pretty fishmonger a suspicious glance. "But how can she tell who casts the most money?"

Another man in a patched shirt looked very sad. "But I'm very poor, and so I'll never have a chance to marry her."

A third one burst into laughter. "The basket is so big, how can one miss?"

The men could not wait to untie their purses and toss copper, silver, and gold coins into the fishmonger's basket. But something strange happened. None of the money reached the basket. As if all the coins had eyes and were distracted by the fishmonger's dazzling beauty, they landed all over the ground instead.

A year later, a magnificent bridge had been built across the Luoyang River.

The Dragon King, although he could still stir waves, could no longer have the pleasure of dunking people. When he saw all the children with their mothers and fathers, grandmothers and grandfathers, and cats and dogs walking happily across the bridge, he felt so defeated that he even lost his power to make waves.

The Mouse Bride

Once upon a time in China, some mice lived happily in their own village. Not only was this little village famous for the piles of delicious food that the mice had stored up, but also and most of all, for the beautiful daughter of the Mayor. But neither of these things made the Mayor happy.

One day when Ming Ming, a boy mouse, passed by the Mayor's mansion, he caught the Mayor looking up at the sky and shaking his head. "My daughter is so beautiful and talented, yet she is so strong-willed," the Mayor sighed and as he frowned, his thick brows knitted into two wriggling worms, "I wonder who can be strong and good enough to be her husband?"

Just as Ming Ming was about to say, "Sir, I am strong and brave," suddenly the fluffy tail of a huge cat flicked against the wall. In no time, Ming Ming and the Mayor scurried into separate holes.

Two days later on a sunny day, big posters were seen pasted on pillars and walls all over the village:

Husband wanted

A young mouse is wanted to be my daughter's husband. On the first day of December, anyone who is handsome and strong, please come to my mansion. My daughter will throw her embroidered handkerchief from the balcony, and whoever has the fastest kung fu moves and jumps the highest to catch it will be her bridegroom.

The Mayor

A crowd gathered to read the announcement and once the mice had finished reading, the excited crowd burst into cheers. Then they began to boast to each other. One plump mouse tilted up his chin and sneered. "Of course I'll be the bridegroom," he said proudly while pushing up the muscle on his arm. "Look, who can possibly have bigger muscles than me?" He laughed so heartily as if he had just discovered a cave filled with dim sum and sweets.

A tall mouse squeezed forward and pointed his long finger at his rival. "You fatso! Ha! Ha! Ha! Who cares about big muscles? No one here is as tall as I am! Look, I have the longest legs and I will jump the highest and catch the handkerchief!"

The smaller mice could only lower their heads in shame and tuck their tails defeatedly between their little legs. From a corner Ming Ming watched, all the while smiling hopefully. And so a week later, hundreds of mice, all dressed in their best kung fu outfits, pushed and shoved and elbowed their way to the courtyard of the Mayor's mansion. The Mayor's beautiful daughter Mei Mei, blushing like a bride, came out onto the balcony. The crowd whistled and cheered, their applause shaking the ground like an earthquake. Mei Mei looked shyly at her suitors. Then, with her delicate hand, she threw the pink handkerchief.

Just as the tallest mouse was about to grab the fluttering handkerchief, a loud "Meeeoww!" startled everyone. Before anyone knew what had happened, a huge spotted cat leapt toward the tiny balcony, stretched his paw and hooked the handkerchief. As the cat fell, it knocked down the whole mansion, smashing it into little pieces. None of the mice wanted to be the cat's meal, so they ran as fast as if the sky were pouring boiling rain. Everyone except Ming Ming. Instead of scurrying away, he shrieked and dashed up to Mei Mei, grabbed her paw, and disappeared with her into a hole.

The next day the Mayor woke up in the rubble of his house. Feeling dazed, he looked for his daughter but she was nowhere to be found. But he comforted himself by thinking, "I saw her running into a hole, so she must have escaped and will soon come back to me."

Just then, the sun rose high up in the sky and shone on his sorrowful face. Feeling its warmth, he murmured to himself, "The sun gives out light to keep us from the cold and help things grow. I can't think of anything more powerful than the sun, nor more worthy to be my son-in-law."

Having decided, he climbed to the top of a wall, shaded his eyes and asked, "Mr. Hot Sun, are you the most powerful of all? If you are, you'll be my son-in-law."

Looking very happy, the sun exclaimed, "Wow! What an unexpected offer!" Just then a dark cloud lunged forward and shaded the sun's brilliant face.

Shocked, the Mayor exclaimed, "It's you! Mr. Dark Cloud!" Dark Cloud laughed so hard that he choked. "Ha, Ha, Harrr... Didn't you notice that when the sun sees me, he's like a mouse seeing a cat?"

When the Mayor was about to bow to Dark Cloud, a strong wind jumped high in the sky and kicked the cloud away!

Now the Mayor snapped his head around. "Wow! Mr. Cold Wind, you've just wiped the cloud clean!"

Cold Wind roared, "Sure! I can blow anything clean, houses, people—and you!" With cheeks swollen like two balloons, he blew his breath on the Mayor.

The mouse soared into mid-air, limbs flailing in all directions. "Aii-ya! Help! Help!"

A few seconds later, he hit the wall with a thump, then his bottom crashed onto a heap of rubble. Recovering from his fall, he looked up at the smiling wall with awe. "Ah, Mr. Tall Wall, so you're the strongest of all!" But the wall's smile disappeared as quickly as it had come.

Puzzled, the Mayor asked, "What's wrong Mr. Tall Wall? Aren't you the most powerful of all?"

But now the wall looked so scared that he was unable to talk. He kept looking at one spot—a mouse peeking out from a hole. Finally, the wall stuttered, "Yes, I'm fearless, except for one thing— mice chewing holes in my stomach!" The Mayor followed the wall's eyes until he saw Ming Ming, and to his surprise and happiness, Mei Mei.

He dashed up to hug his precious daughter. "Mei Mei, where have you been? I worried about you till my heart broke!"

Mei Mei cast a long loving look toward Ming Ming and tenderly said, "Father, yesterday Ming Ming saved my life from the spotted cat." She paused, her face as pink as a peach. "Not only that, when Ming Ming loudly shrieked, the cat dropped my handkerchief and he grabbed it just in time before we ran away."

"Is that so?" The Mayor stared at the couple in disbelief. "Father, don't you see that we're safe and sound?" said Mei Mei. The Mayor turned to Ming Ming with a look of newfound respect. Mei Mei's face was now beaming with happiness and looked as beautiful as sparkling dew on a flower.

A month later, on New Year's day, there was a big wedding procession—the grandest the mouse village had ever known. It was all for Mei Mei and Ming Ming—the most beautiful girl and the bravest boy in the mouse village.

Every year since then, Chinese place bits of sesame, candy, and corn into holes and under their beds as New Year's gifts for mice—so that they will be busy celebrating Mei Mei's and Ming Ming's wedding anniversary and not eat the villagers' food.

22

Dream of the Butterfly

The weather was warm and the wind blew as lazily as a dog wagging its tail while dreaming of a bone. Under the cool shade of bamboo trees, Zhuang Zi, a learned scholar, dozed off and had a dream. In this strange dream, he was no longer a scholar, but a butterfly.

"Fluuup! Fluuup! Fluuup!" His colorful wings swayed this way and that in the cool breeze. His heavy scholar's robe left behind on the ground, Zhuang Zi's body was now as light as a feather. Wings as thin as kites replaced his once long, bulky sleeves. As a lovely butterfly, Zhuang Zi soared higher and higher up into the sky, lifted on the wind until he reached the clouds. Then he looked down at the world below glittering like diamonds.

The former scholar was dizzy with happiness. "Waaahh! How wonderful it is to be a butterfly!" he exclaimed. He had completely forgotten that he had once been Zhuang Zi, the scholar who never looked up at the sky because he always cast his eyes down on his many books, papers, brushes, and ink stones.

"Fluuup! Fluuup! Fluuup!" Far, far he soared, gliding over mountaintops where snow never melted; over houses as small as toys, with children playing outside who looked as small as tiny beetles; over islands shaped like turtle shells; over the sea as green as the tea he drank to fight sleep so that he could read and read.

"Ha!" He felt the wind sweeping past him, swelling his wings like sails. "It's so nice to be a butterfly, so light and so free!"

On and on he flew, past stars like snowflakes; past the moon, yellow as a giant egg yolk. He was almost at the end of the Milky Way, white as rabbit's fur.

Suddenly, a strong gust of wind rustled through the bamboo grove. One leaf snapped off from its branch and fell right on the sleeping scholar's head. It bounced onto his nose, across his cheek, and down his neck before finally landing on his hand. Feeling the leaf tickle him, Zhuang Zi woke up. He brushed the leaf away, only to be surprised by the weight of his long-sleeved arm. Puzzled and groggy, he lifted both arms and gave them a long look.

"Didn't I have wings?" he asked aloud.

The only reply was the rustling of the bamboo leaves, making a "Shaaa! Shaaa!" sound as if to say, "Yes! Yes!"

Zhuang Zi waved his hands this way and that, hoping that the beautiful wings would grow back from his long sleeves. But what he saw was nothing other than his long, bony hands.

"What happened?" he cried. "Wasn't I a butterfly a minute ago?"

"Shaaa! Shaaa!" The bamboo leaves rustled again, but this time they seemed to say, "No! No!"

To calm himself, Zhuang Zi looked around the peaceful garden—at the leaves swaying in rhythm with the breeze; the peaches ripening on the trees; the water rippling on the pond, all the while listening to the pleasant cries of the cicadas....

"Ah, who am I? Am I Zhuang Zi dreaming of being a butterfly, or am I a butterfly dreaming of being Zhuang Zi?" Moments passed, and again he asked himself the same question, "Am I me, or am I a butterfly?"

Zhuang Zi fell into deep thought and then he began to understand—whether he was Zhuang Zi or a beautiful butterfly, he could always enjoy the world of nature around him.

The Cowherd and the Spinning Girl

Once upon a time in China, an orphan boy lived with his mean brother and his brother's even meaner wife. Although the boy was hard-working, smart and honest, he was hated in the family for eating one more bowl of rice and taking up one more bed. Every day before sunrise, he was kicked out of the house to herd the cows. And that was how he got the nickname, "Cowherd."

Cowherd had barely grown from a boy to a man when he was pushed out the door again, this time forever. The brother and his wife gave him only a filthy, broken-down cottage and an old, sick, yellow cow. But Cowherd never complained. Instead, he cleaned up the hut as best he could, tended to the cow with herbs and dew that he collected, and lived happily herding and chopping wood.

One day when Cowherd was out on the mountain gathering twigs, the old cow led him farther and farther into a nearby forest. Soon they reached an opening where

brooks babbled cheerily and colorful birds chirped. While Cowherd was enjoying the scene, eight fairies riding on fragrant clouds suddenly descended to the river bank. Quickly, Cowherd pulled his old cow and himself behind an ancient tree to hide. The fairies took off their five-colored robes and plunged into the jade river. In the rippling water they played, giggled, swam, and splashed each other. Cowherd was completely fascinated by the happy fairies, especially the youngest one who had the longest and softest hair cascading like a beautiful waterfall.

Suddenly the old cow spoke, startling him, "That one is the heavenly weaver. If you want her to be your wife, you must snatch her robe."

Cowherd stared at the old cow in disbelief.

"Hurry before the sun sets and they fly back to heaven." The cow's normally dull eyes twinkled. "Take her robe and make her your wife. Quick!"

Then, with a wobbly leg, the aged beast gave its master a heavy kick.

Cowherd stumbled out from behind the tree, tiptoed to the jade river, and snatched up the youngest fairy's robe. When the sun started to set, one by one the fairies retrieved their clothes and floated back to heaven on their fragrant clouds. All except the youngest one with the longest, blackest hair. She looked and looked but could not find her robe.

"Oh heavens, what happened? I am sure I put it right here next to the river!" Her body trembling in the water, she started to cry. "Oh, what am I going to do? I can't go back if I don't find my clothes, and Father will be very angry."

Just then Cowherd came out from behind the tree, walked up to the fairy, and returned her five-colored robe. His face shining with tender love, he timidly asked, "Fair weaver, would you be my wife?"

Sensing that Cowherd was honest, strong and loving, the fairy blushed while her long hair trembled like soft rippling waves. Then she nodded gracefully like a flower in the spring wind. The two became husband and wife in a ceremony performed by the old cow and witnessed by the jade river.

A year later, on the seventh day of the seventh month, the fairy gave birth to a boy and a girl. Besides taking care of her children, she also taught the village girls how to raise silkworms, spin the thread, and weave it into the softest and smoothest cloth. With magical hands, she spun rolls of silk that shone like rainbows. The villagers discovered that the clothes she made kept them cool in summer and warm in winter. They took to calling her Spinning Girl and more and more villagers came to her begging to learn her weaving skill.

Soon Spinning Girl's fame spread to heaven and reached the ears of her father, the Heavenly Emperor. Furious that she had not returned to heaven, the Emperor ordered the Heavenly Empress, together with the Heavenly Troops, to descend to earth to look for her.

One day when Cowherd was plowing with his old cow, a sudden roar slashed the sky like thunder. The old cow raised her head, then spoke to her master. "I fear something bad is going to happen." Her face streaked with tears, the old cow went on, "The heavenly drums are beating. The Heavenly Empress and her Heavenly Troops are coming to take your wife away!"

Cowherd threw down his plow and dashed home. But he was too late. The Heavenly Empress and her soldiers had already seized Spinning Girl. Swiftly, Cowherd put his children in two baskets and ran after the Heavenly Troops, screaming, "Please let my wife go, please!"

The children, tears streaming and limbs flailing, yelled at the tops of their small voices, "Mama! Mama! Please come back! Please!"

Spinning Girl tried to reach out to her children, but she was already far up in the sky. The angry Heavenly Empress snatched out a hairpin and threw it in front of Cowherd and the two children. As the pin sailed through the air, the sky split with a deafening roar and a wide river gushed through a huge hole in the clouds. The waves rose so high and roared so loud that Cowherd and the children were unable to follow their mother to the realm of the Heavenly Emperor and Empress.

From then on, the grief-stricken Cowherd stood on the east side of the heavenly river while the heart-broken Spinning Girl stood on the west.

Day and night husband and wife stared longingly at each other with tears in their eyes. The children nestled against their father and cried and cried.

One day their cries reached the ears of the Heavenly Emperor. Taking pity on the lonely children, he consented for the couple to meet on the seventh day of the seventh month every year—the children's birthday. A flock of magpies, moved by the couple's undying love and loyalty, flew over the river and formed a bridge by holding each other's tail. And so every year, the family celebrates their joyful reunion in the middle of the bridge of magpies.

Ever since, in China, women and girls make offerings of food and wine to Cowherd and Spinning Girl on the seventh day of the seventh month, praying for a love as true as theirs.

The Ghost Catcher

An emperor named Xuan Zong once ruled China. Several times a year, he would travel about his empire to carry out his duties—inspecting the royal troops, performing many rituals for heaven and earth, and generally checking up on everyone.

One day, after Xuan Zong had returned from one of his long trips, he fell sick. The fever lasted a month. His cheeks glowed hot like burning coals, and his head felt as if it were going to explode. The imperial doctors and priests tried many things to cure him—rare herbs, hearty soups, perfumed incense, magic writing, even offerings to put out the fire of heaven's anger—but nothing worked. Finally, they decided there was only one cure—sleep. So the emperor spent most of his time asleep in his luxurious bed decorated with the finest silk-embroidered curtains and gold pillars.

One night, after he had finished eating a big bowl of hot and tasty chicken soup, Xuan Zong fell asleep and entered dreamworld. He soon spotted a flickering shadow—a ghost! The ghost had no feet; his tiny body was covered with rags, and a fan dangled from his waist. Xuan Zong was surprised that this little imp of a ghost did not bow deeply to him like everybody else. As the emperor was about to scold him for his rudeness, the ghost reached out his sharp-nailed fingers and snatched the emperor's most precious possessions: jade flute, jeweled crown, even his heavy gold ingots and coins.

"Hee! Hee! Heee!" The ghost laughed, tilting his pointy-eared head from side to side while floating toward the door.

"Stop!" Xuan Zong shot up from his bed. "Who are you?"

The figure smiled cunningly. "I'm a ghost, and my name is Empty Waste. I like to empty people's pockets and waste their money. Hee! Hee! Heee!"

Cheeks red with anger, Xuan Zong yelled, "Stop! Don't you dare go away!" Then he looked around and screamed at the top of his voice, "Guards! Soldiers! Help! Help! Come catch this little ghost!"

But instead of seeing scores of armed men coming to his rescue, the emperor saw another, larger ghost approach. This one had a bandaged head, was wrapped in a long robe and wore heavy boots. Before Xuan Zong had a chance to scream, he was shocked to see Big Ghost chase Little Ghost round and round in circles, then snatch him up and pop him into his long-toothed mouth.

The emperor's body was now shaking like an earthquake. "Who are you and where are you from?" he asked.

Big Ghost bowed. "Your Majesty, I am Zhong Kui from the South Mountain. I once led a happy life as a student in your world. But then tragedy struck: I failed the imperial examination. I was so humiliated that I killed myself by hitting my head on the steps of the examination hall. Your kind father took pity on me and gave me a proper burial. My spirit is forever indebted to him. So from that day on, I swore I would devour all the bad ghosts and restore peace to the empire." Zhong Kui bowed again to the emperor. "Here are Your Majesty's precious possessions." Big Ghost opened his hand which held the emperor's jade flute, jeweled crown, heavy gold ingots, and coins.

The emperor was about to reach out to take them when he woke up.

Xuan Zong was astonished to find that his sickness had vanished like the morning dew. "Good heavens, can this be true? That horrible little ghost was causing my sickness and the good ghost Zhong Kui got rid of him for me."

To celebrate his return to good health, Xuan Zong asked his court painter, Wu, to paint scenes of the two ghosts whom he had seen in his dream. Because Wu was the greatest painter in China, he was able to finish the painting in a single day.

After Wu presented the picture to Xuan Zong, the emperor studied it, then looked down at the court painter. "Did you have the same dream as I? This is exactly what I saw!"

Wu bowed deeply. "Your Majesty wasn't the only one terrorized by the ghost known as Empty Waste; many of your subjects have lost valuable possessions to this ghost, myself included. But thanks to your father's kindness, the good ghost Zhong Kui has saved us all."

Wu smiled politely and went on, "But guarding the dreams of the emperor is a very large task for one ghost. Now that Your Majesty has this painting, it will protect you, and Zhong Kui will not have to work so hard."

"I see." The emperor stroked his beard thoughtfully. "So every night I will sleep well and have sweet dreams?"

"I'm sure you will, Your Majesty."

And the emperor did.

Ever since, "ghost-catcher" paintings have been very popular in China, where people hang them up to scare away the bad ghosts.

The Frog Who Lived in a Well

Sitting in the well and looking at the sky is an old proverb. The Chinese use it to describe people who think they know everything but actually know very little.

For example, there once was a frog who lived inside a well shaped like a deep wok. The frog was so happy with his home that he always boasted to his many friends—tiny crabs, fish, bugs, tadpoles, dragonflies, and worms—how wonderful the well was.

"Look," he said to a crab as he tilted up his head, "the sky looks so bright and clear from here, and so round! No place is better than my well."

Another time he cast a delighted look at a tadpole, while flinging his limbs in the water this way and that. "See, there's so much water here for us to play in! No place is better than my well."

But his friends soon grew tired of his constant boasting. They began to ignore him and went about their own business. One day a big turtle from the Eastern Ocean crawled past the well. Frog was sitting on a ledge near the wall appreciating the sky when he spotted this unexpected visitor.

"Hi there!" Frog yelled. "What a rare guest! Please, my friend, please come pay me a visit!"

Big Turtle looked down inside the small well, straining his eyes. "Hi! How's life down there? It can't be very comfortable, can it?"

Frog looked up, his eyes bulging, his tone annoyed. "What a thing to say! Of course it's comfortable down here. In fact, it's wonderful!"

Big Turtle cast a doubtful look down the narrow opening. "Is that so?"

Frog went on excitedly, "This well is all mine. There's plenty of water to quench my thirst and I can float all day long if I want to. I live like a king, so how could I not be comfortable?"

Before Big Turtle could reply, Frog splashed the water with his short limbs. "See what I can do?" He began somersaulting and diving. Finally his head emerged, his bulging eyes sparkling with delight. "Guess what? I've just had my feet massaged by the soft mud at the bottom of the well!"

Big Turtle smiled at his newly met friend. "So you think life's pretty great in your well, huh?"

Frog smiled back. "Sure. At night, when I'm tired of swimming, I'll hop along the wall, waking up my friends to say hello. Then I'll take a nap floating on a leaf and dream strange dreams. So, what more can a bulge-eyed creature ask for? I'm the king of the well, ha, ha, ha!" He gave Big Turtle a triumphant look. "So, why don't you come down and take a look at my kingdom?"

"All right," said Big Turtle. But the closer he got to the well, the smaller the

opening looked. "I'm sorry, Frog. I don't think I can make it down there."

"Why not?" Frog asked, his voice sounding very sad and his face looking like a deflated balloon.

"I'm too big. The opening of your well is far too small for me to fit through. I don't want to get stuck."

Frog eyed his friend through the well's opening. "You don't look very big to me."

"That's because the opening is so small, you can only see my face. You haven't yet seen my long neck, my strong shell, or my sturdy legs." Before Frog could say anything more, Big Turtle went on, "Of course, I'm no where near as big as most of my other friends from the Eastern Ocean. Compared to them I'm small!"

Frog's eyes bulged even more. "You mean there are creatures out there that are bigger than you?"

"Much bigger! Shall I tell you how big the Eastern Ocean is?" Big Turtle said.

"Okay," Frog laughed. "But it can't be much bigger than my well." Then he hopped onto a tiny leaf, crossed his legs comfortably, and waited for Big Turtle to begin.

"The Eastern Ocean is so big that no one can tell how wide or how deep it is. In ancient times, during Emperor Yu's rule, there were floods for nine years but the water in the Eastern Ocean never rose. During old Emperor Shun's rule, no rain fell for seven years, but the water in the Eastern Ocean never went down. The Eastern Ocean is so big that nothing can change it."

Big Turtle looked down at his tiny friend. "That's why I am proud to live there."

The frog was struck speechless by the vastness of the Eastern Ocean. He even fell off his leaf and sank almost to the bottom of the well before he could get over his shock. Then he climbed back on his leaf, a little unsteadily. He stared at Big Turtle for a moment, then spoke timidly, "Really, is that so? I think you made up this Eastern Ocean."

Big Turtle smiled. "Then I'll show it to you. But first you have to hop out of this little well you live in."

Straight away Frog used all his might to hop. One! Two! Three! Four! Finally he was able to jump out of the well and land on the soft moss at the top.

"Waaahh!" he exclaimed, swinging his head and shading his eyes.

Big Turtle asked, "Is there something wrong, my friend?"

"Aeeeii!" Frog shouted, his face flushed and his head dizzy from the sun.

"Are you sure you're all right, little friend?" Big Turtle asked.

Sweating heavily, Frog nodded. "I always thought that the sky was round and that it was the size of my well's opening. I never knew that it was so huge—I can't even see its edge!"

Before Big Turtle could say anything, Frog exclaimed, "And the sun! It blinds my eyes! I never knew it was so powerful!"

"Calm down, my friend," Big Turtle said gently. "Now do you understand why I said the well is small? Certainly your well is a great place to live, but there are many great places on the earth—some much greater than your well."

Very embarrassed, Frog just hung his head. He would still enjoy his life in the well, but now he knew that he—and his well—were just a small part of an incredibly big world....

Chang-E Flies to the Moon

Do you ever wonder why there is only one sun in the sky? In ancient China you could see ten! All ten had yellow faces and red hair; they were brothers, sons of the Heaven King. But they were mean. Each day, they would rise up in the sky and scorch everything—the land, the sea, the people, the animals—even the fish. The Heaven King knew of his sons' nastiness but he had no idea what to do

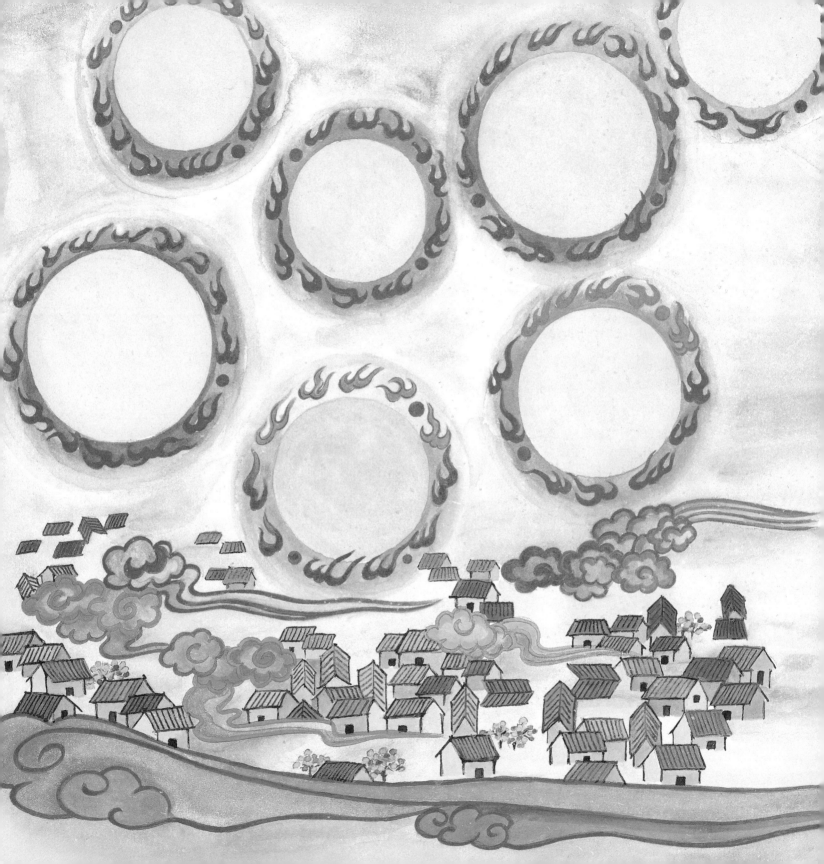

about it. Finally, he decided to send Hou Yi, the heavenly warrior god, down to earth to save it from the horrible heat. But Hou Yi was unwilling to leave his beautiful wife Chang-E. After he sorrowfully explained the king's order to her, she smiled kindly. "Don't worry, my dear husband." The corners of Hou Yi's lips began to lift like sails in the wind when Chang-E spoke again, "I'm your wife, and my duty is to take care of you wherever you are." She chuckled. "Haven't you heard of the saying 'marry a chicken, follow a chicken; marry a dog, follow a dog; marry a monkey, hold onto his tail and jump after him up mountains and down valleys?'"

Soon the couple had settled on earth, and Hou Yi set about carrying out his duty. He looked up at the sky and pleaded to the ten suns, "Instead of circling in the sky at the same time, can't you shine one at a time?"

The ten brothers laughed at the warrior god. They swung closer and closer to earth, burning up more and more land. Forests became ovens, cows became burgers, pigs turned into roasts, chickens began to fry, and people ended up like crisp fried spring rolls.

"What am I going to do now?" Hou Yi's brows furrowed into two heavy hills. "Here I'm supposed to save the earth from burning, but now it's turning into a fireball instead!"

Chang-E put a tender hand on her husband's sore shoulder. "My dear husband, if the suns won't listen to your kind words..." She paused. Suddenly her eyes turned sharp. "Then you had better shoot them down."

The next day, Hou Yi put on warrior's clothes and thick boots, then dashed up to the mountaintop. Shading his eyes, he watched one last time as the suns swept around, spitting balls of flame, while casting triumphant glances at him. As the ten fiery orbs were spinning like giant wheels, Hou Yi took out his bow, slid in a magic arrow, aimed, and began to shoot.

One by one, nine of the suns fell into the ocean. "Zzzuusszzz!" each hissed as his

light went out. Only the tenth sun was now left. He lowered his eyes and pleaded to the mighty archer, "Please Hou Yi, we were wrong. It was just a silly game. I beg you, don't shoot me down. I promise I'll behave."

The last sun kept his promise. From that day on, the single sun left in the sky nurtured the earth during the daytime and hid at night so that everyone could have a peaceful sleep.

Everybody was completely overjoyed, except the Heaven King, who grieved the loss of his nine sons. To punish Hou Yi, he forbade the couple to return to their home in heaven.

Though he thought the Heaven King's order unfair, the warrior god willingly stayed on earth so that he could carry out his other duties. Every day he went out to fight the six monsters: slithering snakes, wild boars, man-eating birds, giant cats, crooked-toothed ogres, and nine-headed fiends. Because of these heroic deeds, Hou Yi became more and more popular each day he spent on earth. But his wife Chang-E grew sadder and sadder.

One day, tears streaming down her face, Chang-E said to Hou Yi, "My dear husband, I really miss heaven and I want to go back."

While Hou Yi loved his fame on earth, he loved his pretty wife even more. He thought for a while. "All right, let's make a sacrifice of the six monsters to please the Heaven King."

Slithering snakes, wild boars, man-eating birds, giant cats, crooked-toothed ogres, and the nine-headed fiends were placed on the altar with burning incense which carried the couple's prayers all the way to heaven. But the Heaven King blew out the incense and covered his ears. He could never forgive Hou Yi for shooting down his nine sons.

So unhappy to be stuck on earth, Chang-E began to pick fights with Hou Yi.

At first the fights were every month, then every week, and finally every day. Everytime Chang-E complained about her husband's stupidity in shooting down the suns and offending the Heaven King.

In turn, Hou Yi reminded his wife that it was she who had come up with the idea. The quarrels between husband and wife continued from sunrise to sunset, then again from sunset to sunrise.

Finally, Hou Yi was so fed up that he left home. He decided to ask for advice from the Queen Mother of the West who lived on Kunlun Mountain. When he arrived there, however, he found her fast asleep. Not wanting to come away empty-handed, Hou Yi snatched her immortality pills. Once back home, he tucked the pills inside a drawer and then forgot about them.

Days and months passed. Chang-E became more and more bored with her life on earth. How she missed all the beautiful music and dancing in heaven, the good food, and the worry-free days!

One day when Hou Yi was out hunting, Chang-E started to search for something to amuse herself with. Suddenly, she discovered the immortality pills. While the pills rolled around in her palms, her heart pounded like a pestle hitting a mortar. Maybe, she thought, I should just take the pills and leave Hou Yi.

The neighing of horses aroused Chang-E from her thoughts. She lifted her head and saw her husband's tired face coming toward the house. In an instant, she popped all the pills into her mouth and stepped outside to meet him. Then, when Hou Yi was just twenty steps from her, Chang-E's body began to lift higher and higher, like a soaring kite. Tears rolled down the warrior's cheeks as he tried to reach for his wife, who soon turned into a dot vanishing in the vast blue sky.

When Chang-E neared heaven, to her surprise, the guardians of the heavenly gate blocked her way.

"Why?" She asked with disbelief.

"Because you left your husband! That's not the behavior of a good wife!" Their words roared like thunder, splitting Chang-E's ears. "A good wife and husband should share each other's joy and pain!"

Since Chang-E could not get into Heaven nor return to Earth, she ended up living on the Moon. Her only company was a lively jade rabbit who kept pounding a mortar to make immortality pills.

"These pills are a constant reminder of my mistake," Chang-E would sigh, while thinking of Hou Yi and regretting her selfishness.

Back on earth, Hou Yi would look up at the moon every night, tie a love letter for his wife onto an arrow, raise his bow, and release the arrow. But the bow had lost its magic. No matter how hard the warrior god pulled, the arrow traveled only a short distance before falling to earth. But each night he would try again. For Hou Yi still loved his wife very much.

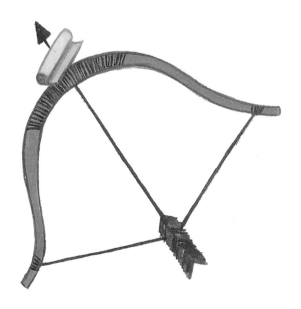

The Wolf and the Scholar

Once upon a time, there lived a scholar named Dongguo, who was known for being gentle and kind. Dongguo loved to read, so one day he visited a bookseller and bought many books. When he was hauling his heavy bag home along a tree-lined road, he spotted a wolf running in his direction. Immediately, Dongguo moved aside to let the animal pass. But to his surprise, the wolf stopped right in front of him.

The wolf knelt down and kowtowed. "Honorable master, please help me!"

"Is something wrong?" Dongguo asked gently.

The wolf took a deep breath and blurted out, "Master, I'm being chased by a troop of hunters. Believe me, when they catch me, they'll chop me into pieces, fry me in their sizzling wok, pop my shredded body into their mouth, then spit out my crunched bones! I don't want them to eat me! So please help!"

The scholar eyed the wolf kindly. "Of course I'll help you. First, calm down. Then tell me what I can do."

"Good master," the wolf smiled, casting a look at Dongguo's large bag, "you can hide me in your bag and when the hunters come and ask about me, just tell them you haven't seen anyone."

Immediately the kind-hearted scholar opened his bag, pushed aside his new books, and let the wolf get in. After that, he set the bag back on his shoulder.

Just then the group of hunters arrived. There were six of them, each carrying a quiver with several sharp arrows sticking out. One tall and muscular hunter went up to Dongguo, put his hands together in a gesture of respect and said politely, "Honorable scholar, did you happen to see a wolf?"

Dongguo pretended to think for a while. "Yes," he said, and then pointed to the forest at the far end of the road. "I saw it dash into the woods. Why don't you go there and look?"

"What a good idea." The hunter smiled. "Thank you for your precious time, honorable scholar."

After Dongguo made sure that the last hunter had disappeared inside the woods, he untied his bag and let the wolf out.

The wolf smiled, this time baring his long, sharp fangs. "I am most grateful that you saved my life. However, since you're well known for being kind-hearted," the wolf cast the scholar a cunning look, "would you save my life a second time?"

Dongguo looked around, puzzled. "What do you mean? Don't you see that the hunters have all gone and that you're safe now?"

"Ha! Ha! I don't mean that, my dear scholar."

"Then what do you mean?"

The wolf rose tall to whisper into Dongguo's ear, "All right, let me be honest with you. I'm now very, very hungry. I haven't even had so much as a rabbit's ear or a monkey's tail in my stomach for three days, which means...." The wolf flicked his long, pink tongue across the scholar's cheek. "... Which means that I want to eat you, right now."

Dongguo almost fell over. "You want to—?"

Wolf cut him off. "Otherwise I'll starve. Is that what you want? I thought you were famous for being kind. So, are you kind or not?"

Just when the wolf was about to fall upon the scholar, an old man passed by. He noticed Dungguo's terrified expression and asked, "My friends, are you two all right?"

Dongguo seized the chance to explain the whole thing to the old man. Before finishing, he added, "Mister, please tell the wolf that he's wrong!"

Before the old man had a chance to talk, the wolf was already speaking, "Sir, what this scholar told you was a complete lie!"

"Is that so? Why don't you tell me your side of the story?" said the old man.

The wolf began to talk, looking very dejected, "He didn't save my life. Instead, he tried to kill me! First, he bound my feet so I couldn't move, then he pushed me inside that small bag. After that, he piled his books on top of me to crush my bones. Worse, he tied the bag as tightly as he could to squeeze out the air, so that I almost died." The wolf now looked more pitiful than ever. "Sir, please believe me. This scholar always pretends to be kind so people fall for his tricks but he's really terribly cruel!"

"All right, all right." The old man waved his bony hand to quiet the wolf. "I'll only believe you if you can prove how the scholar tried to kill you. Why don't you jump into the bag again and show me what happened?"

"Okay," the wolf said, and crawled inside the bag in no time.

The old man immediately tied the bag and tightened it as best as he could. He asked Dongguo, "Do you have a knife?"

"A knife?" The scholar looked horrified. "Please don't tell me you're going to kill the wolf!"

The old man quickly retorted, "Would you rather let him escape and try to eat you again?"

"No. But...." Dongguo stammered.

"Come on, give me your knife!" The old man waved his hand frantically.

Dongguo stammered more, "...I...don't carry a knife."

"All right," the old man said, then tried to strangle the wolf with his bare hands.

The scholar yelled, "Good heavens, you're hurting him!"

"Ha! Of course I'm hurting him!" The old man tilted his head and laughed. "Scholar, you surely have a kind heart, but you're also very stupid."

"Being kind is not stupid."

As the two were arguing, the wolf spoke from inside the bag. "Kind gentlemen, the scholar did try to save my life. I lied and I was wrong. So can you two spare my life one more time?"

Before the old man had a chance to stop him, the scholar had already untied the bag and let the wolf out.

Tears streaming down his face, the wolf bowed down and kowtowed, this time with sincerity. "Kind-hearted masters, forgive my cunning. I have learned much from the scholar; I promise that from now on I will behave."

After the wolf had gone, the old man said to the scholar, "I hope you're right about that wolf."

Dongguo smiled. "Being kind is always right."

Playing the Qin for the Water Buffalo

In ancient China, people admired the soft and soothing sounds of the *qin* more than any other musical instrument. The *qin* is a zither, made of a special paulownia wood on which are stretched seven silk strings.

Once upon a time, the emperor's favorite musician was a *qin* player called Mingyi. Mingyi very much enjoyed playing beautiful music to the emperor, empress, princes, princesses, ministers, lords and ladies, and all the pretty and handsome dancers. When his fingers glided along the *qin,* the dancers would match the movements by sweeping their long sleeves like brush strokes. And while his fingers moved elegantly along the silk strings, the dancers would rise into the air effortlessly like colorful kites. Then the emperor, empress, the princes and princesses, and all the other noble guests would loudly clap and repeatedly cheer and shout, "Wonderful! Wonderful!"

When Mingyi finished, the emperor would pour Mingyi's favorite drink into a bronze cup and place it before him along with the tastiest food—roasted pig, drunken shrimp, sugar and vinegar fish, scallion chicken soaked in oil.

"Mingyi," the emperor would say, smoothing his beard, "when I listen to your beautiful music, all my worries vanish like the morning dew!" Overjoyed with happiness, Mingyi would bow deeply with his head touching his knees, thank the emperor with words sweeter than his music, then drink and gobble down his food. After that, he would play the emperor's favorite pieces, one after another. Tunes like *Happy Spring* and *White Snow, High Mountain and Flowing Water,* and *Fisherman's Song* would flow smoothly from his fingertips—and always brought joyful tears and thunderous applause.

One day after Mingyi had finished playing in the royal court, he decided to relax by taking a walk in the imperial garden. It was spring. The breeze was soothing like caressing hands and the grass was green as an emerald sea. He spotted an ancient tree and quickly went to sit under its branches. "Ah, what a nice place to play my

instrument!" Mingyi exclaimed, taking his *qin* out from its silk case and starting to play. Just as his fingers began stroking the strings, a water buffalo ambled toward him. Excited, he stopped playing to study the beast, then stroked his chin and smiled. "Ah, even a water buffalo can enjoy my music. How wonderful!"

Knowing that this was an audience harder to impress than his noble guests, Mingyi used all his musical skill. He swayed his fingers this way and that. At first they resembled little fish wiggling their tails; then dragonflies skipping on water; finally, phoenixes soaring in the sky.

After playing for a while, Mingyi noticed, to his disappointment, that the water buffalo was more interested in munching grass than listening to the beautiful tunes flowing from his fingers.

Annoyed, Mingyi stopped playing music and started banging on the *qin's* strings.

To his utter surprise, the water buffalo stopped eating, looked up from the grass, then cheerfully flicked his tail and swayed his head to the tuneless twangs.

Mingyi suddenly realized that the water buffalo had mistaken the twangs for a grasshopper's buzz—and that this was more entertaining to the beast than the playing of a great musician!

Mingyi cast a bitter look at his audience. "You have no idea what good music sounds like, do you?"

The water buffalo just stared back with blank eyes and started to eat again.

Feeling even more upset, Mingyi again banged hard on the *qin*. "All right," he shouted, "if this is what you like to hear!" His fingers struck the strings in a succession of "Twang! Twang! Twang! Twang!"

Instead of being frightened by Mingyi's angry plucking, the water buffalo kept flicking his tail and swaying his head, now looking very cheerful.

The moment Mingyi put down his *qin*, he understood something very interesting about his music. Of course, the sounds of nature are like beautiful music for animals. But the *qin* is made by human beings and its music is for humans to enjoy.

Happy again, Mingyi now began to play for his own pleasure, leaving the water buffalo to enjoy the buzzing of bugs.

Both felt content relaxing under the plum blossom trees, enjoying the gentle breeze, and letting nature's myriad sounds make soothing music in their ears.

Carp Jumping over the Dragon Gate

Along time ago in China, the Yellow River flooded constantly, its angry waves drowning people and animals day after day. The village chief, alarmed at the loss of so many lives, resolved to put a stop to the River God's mischief.

The village workers tried to block the river with big boulders. But the river splashed over the rocks and as the years passed, so many men, women, and children were turned into water spirits that the chief finally admitted defeat. He had no choice but to pass the task onto his son, Yu. Yu decided to see if he could figure out a better way to stop the river. Thirteen years went by and he was still trying to find a way to

channel the flood. Touched by Yu's devotion and taking pity on his loneliness, the heavenly Jade Emperor married his only daughter, Tushan Nu, to the young man. Now the couple could work together—using the Jade Emperor's wedding gifts of a holy plow and a ghostly ax. Putting their heads together, Yu and Tushan Nu came up with an idea—dig a deep gorge to carry the raging water safely away from the village.

Work began the next day. Everyone in the town brought a shovel and pitched in to help dig. The work went on for many months until at last, instead of flooding the village, the water rushed down the gorge into a deep valley.

The disaster of flooding seemed to be solved. To commemorate this great event and to honor the couple who had saved them from the terrible floods, the people built a gate over the river and named it the Yu Gate. But while the people rejoiced, the carp who dwelled in the Yellow River were unhappy. Now the water level was so low that they could not jump back over the rocks to reach their homes. Finally, the carp swarmed to complain to Yu and his wife.

The head fish sounded hurt and angry because he had scraped off many of his scales trying to swim back upstream. "Beware! If you two don't bring the water level back up so that we can return to our homes, we'll get all the carp in the Yellow River to stir the waters and make big waves!"

Yu cast all the fish a disapproving glance. "What kind of behavior is this—ganging up against me, against all the people who suffered from the flood!" He pointed a finger toward the Yu Gate. "If you're truly mighty, jump through the Yu Gate and find your way home!"

Now looking exhausted, the head fish said, "Sir, we have tried that! But with the water so low, it's too high for us to jump over the boulders your father put there. Whenever we try to jump, we hit the rocks and flop back into the water."

Tushan Nu stepped in front of her husband and looked down at the school of fish. It was a very sad sight—ragged scales, chipped jaws, sore eyes, missing whiskers, and split tails. "All right, my fish friends," she said, her voice soft and tender, "let me tell my father, the Jade Emperor, about this and we'll see what he can do."

The next day, Tushan Nu made an announcement to the fish. "My father has proclaimed a reward. Those of you who can jump over the Yu Gate will immediately become dragons. Those who fail will have to be content with being ordinary fish, stuck in the Yellow River."

Hearing this, the carp cheered. One with sparkling golden scales cast a triumphant glance at the others. "Brothers and sisters, take good care of yourselves, for soon I'll be a dragon flying in the sky and will no longer keep you company!"

Ever since, when spring comes, an incredible sight appears near the Yu Gate: thousands of carp swim up to the tall gate and jump. Those who jump high enough turn into dragons, flying away with their fiery tails flashing in the sky. They look down with pity at their old friends who must stay behind in the muddy river, eyes looking longingly skyward, hoping to succeed the next time.

In ancient China, students studied extremely hard before they took the imperial examinations. Those who succeeded would become high government officials. Like the carp turning into soaring dragons, their future would be as bright as the morning sun. The Chinese use this story to explain the rewards of hard work: "Once jumped over the dragon gate, fame and fortune will never come late."

How the Fox Tricked the Tiger

In a great forest in ancient China, there was an enormous tiger who was the king of beasts. When he roared, his voice cracked like thunder and all the animals would flee in terror. When he ate, he devoured food piled as high as pagodas, and the other animals could only hide behind trees, swallowing their saliva back to their empty stomachs. When he yawned, his sharp teeth so terrified any animals who heard him that they would jump over cliffs and crash onto the rocks below.

"Ha! Ha! Ha! Ha! I'm the king of kings!" Tiger declared at the top of his voice. His words bounced off the trees, echoed in the valleys, and even shot up high into the sky.

One time a fox was trotting home after a day's hunting when he found himself face to face with the tiger, who was out looking for a tasty meal. Fox was so stunned at the sight of the huge, fierce face that his feet stuck to the ground like a scared snail's and his heart beat like a tribal drum. As soon as he could, Fox gathered up all his strength and broke into a run.

In an instant, Tiger grabbed Fox's tail with a sharp paw. Fox struggled, thrashing his paws and legs as strongly as he could. "Let me go, please let go!" he screamed and screamed as the forest grew more and more silent.

"Ha! Ha! Ha! Harrrr...arrr." Tiger laughed so hard that he almost choked. Then he pressed his claws deeply into Fox's tail. "Do you know I haven't even had a twisting worm to massage my twitching tummy the whole afternoon? Now my tummy is roaring like thunder! Can't you hear it?" Tiger said as he opened his mouth wide, baring his long teeth which gleamed like daggers.

Just as Fox was about to faint from fear, an idea suddenly came into his cunning mind. He mustered up all his courage to stare deeply into his killer's eyes. "Wait a minute, Tiger."

"Yesss?" Tiger asked lazily, flicking his wet, hot tongue on Fox's cheek. "What are your last words? You little twerp!"

"You cannot eat me!" Fox said, sweating, while trying very hard to stop his legs from breaking into a fox trot.

"Can't eat you? Ha! I do what I want, for I am the king of beasts! Now I'm hungry, so I'll eat."

"You can eat, Tiger, but I'm afraid that you can't eat me."

Tiger tilted his black-striped head down to give his prisoner a curious look. "Why not?" he demanded.

Fox spoke with an air of authority. "Because if you do, you'll upset the Heavenly King." The cunning fox paused for suspense before he went on, "... For he has appointed me the king of beasts."

Upon hearing these words, Tiger felt as angry as if he had just been spat on by a tiny mouse. "Nonsense! Nonsense!" He screamed. "Everyone here knows that I am the king of beasts, not a twerp like you!"

Fox freed a paw to put across his mouth. "Shh...be quiet. You don't want the Heavenly King to hear you talk like that, do you?" Before Tiger could reply, Fox rushed on. "You don't want to disturb the order of heaven by eating me, the king of beasts, do you?"

Now Tiger was genuinely puzzled by what he was hearing. He loosened his hold on Fox by a notch.

Fox took this chance to show off his cunning. "If you don't believe what I've told you, just follow me and you'll see how all the other animals in the forest are terrified of me."

"All right, I'll see about that." Tiger tried to hide the confusion in his voice. "But if you've lied, you know where you'll end up," he roared, tapping his tummy, which was as round as a tub. "Right here!"

The king of beasts finally loosened his grasp to let the fox go free.

The two strolled in the forest. Fox told Tiger, "Let me go first so that all the animals know I'm here. Then you'll see something!" They strutted past trees, rocks, ponds, and brooks. As soon as the other animals—birds, owls, rabbits, deer, monkeys, snakes, and elephants—saw them coming, they screamed, "Aii-ya!" and dashed away.

A rabbit ran as if it had been hit by lightning. A snail struggled along as if he had bound feet. A tortoise rolled over several times as if it were doing circus tricks. After this had gone on for quite some time, Fox stopped and turned around to face the tiger. "Tiger, see how they all run away?" he said triumphantly. "Now do you realize that I am the king of beasts?"

Tiger, looking like he had suddenly lost all his stripes, lowered his head and said, "Yes, now that I see how afraid the animals are of you with my own eyes, I agree that you're the king of beasts."

"Ha! Ha! Ha! Good!" Fox gave a few forced laughs. "So now go back home and don't let me see you again, ever!"

"Yes, sir." Tiger purred, his voice like twigs crushed under giant feet.

As soon as Tiger turned away, Fox ran as fast as if he were being chased by an army of demons!

The Monkey King Turns the Heavenly Palace Upside Down

The monkey Wu Kong is the most beloved of all the characters in Chinese children's stories. Monkey is always mischievous, but he means well and is genuinely sorry when he makes mistakes. Some of the most popular stories about Monkey tell of the naughty things he did before the Buddha made him mend his ways. Here is one of them.

Monkey liked to play all day long. When he was bored and had nothing to do, he would play tricks on anyone he could think of. One day, after he got tired of eating flowers, the naughty monkey decided he would visit the Palace of the Eastern Sea. So he jumped on a wave and rode it for thousands of miles until he reached the palace.

When he got there, he asked the Emperor of the Eastern Sea to give him a wooden staff to play with. The emperor refused, so Monkey pulled out one of the pillars holding up the ceiling of the Imperial Chamber. Using his powerful magic,

he transformed it into a gold rod, and carried it out to the steps of the palace where he used it to practice kung fu. Soon Monkey grew bored. Holding the rod in his paws, he somersaulted toward his home on Flower Fruit Mountain.

Because Monkey had stolen the pillar, the Emperor of the Eastern Sea had to hold up the ceiling of his palace with his thick arms. This made him pretty angry! He shouted after Monkey, "Give me back my pillar, you smelly monkey!"

Monkey just laughed as he traveled the ten thousand miles back home. The emperor screamed himself hoarse, and then sent a messenger to the Jade Emperor. "Please, my lord," his messenger said, "the Palace of the Eastern Sea is falling down because that wicked monkey Wu Kong stole my lord Emperor's pillar. Please send your heavenly troops to capture him!"

But the Jade Emperor had a better idea. The next day, he summoned Monkey and said, "Wu Kong, I'll appoint you the official horse keeper. There'll be one thousand horses under your care. How do you like that?"

"Your Highness," Monkey bowed deeply, "I am most honored to receive such a high rank."

"Very well. Then I appoint you to this high position."

"Whiiiiieeee!" Monkey cheered.

"But first you have to give the Emperor of the Eastern Sea back his pillar."

Monkey threw the gold rod into the air where it changed back into a pillar. Then it sailed all the way across the Eastern Ocean and landed in the palace where it rightfully belonged.

Monkey went right to work caring for the Jade Emperor's horses. He was so proud of himself that he hummed happily all day long.

One day, two officials from the emperor's court invited Monkey to join them for a snack. After the three ate and drank everything in sight, Monkey asked, "Tell me, just how high is my rank of horse keeper?"

His friends burst into uncontrollable laughter. They nudged each other, smirking at Monkey, then one said, "Don't you know? It's the worst job anyone can have!"

Furious, Monkey knocked the two officials down, and dashed out of the palace through the Heaven Gate, bowling over a troop of heavenly soldiers. Monkey had barely gotten home to the Flower Fruit Mountain, when two witches appeared. "Honorable Wu Kong," they said and bowed deeply, "Please don't be so angry! Put this on!" Big smiles bloomed on their faces while they handed Monkey a gorgeous golden robe. "You can be king here on your own mountain." The witches whispered to each other, "Now Monkey will really get in trouble!" And they laughed.

Monkey was so happy that his lips stretched all the way to his ears.

"Wonderful! From now on, I'll be the Monkey King! Let the Jade Emperor find another horse keeper!"

Soon the Jade Emperor heard about the self-crowned king. Furious that someone else dared to call himself king, he immediately sent Giant Spirit and Little Immortal to capture Monkey. The troop of heavenly soldiers descending toward the Flower Fruit Mountain was so large that the stomping of their feet and the beating of their battle drums shook the highest mountains and rippled the widest rivers. Giant Spirit immediately spotted Monkey, who was hanging by his tail from his front porch. Giant Spirit dashed toward him, but before he could swing his ax, Monkey grabbed it and broke it in two!

"Ha!" Monkey cast a triumphant look at his enemy. "Flee for your life before it's too late!"

Little Immortal transformed himself into a three-headed, six-armed Big Immortal and sprinted forward.

"Ha!" Monkey sneered. "Who do you think you are? You little toy!"

Little Immortal screamed, using all three of his voices. "You smelly monkey, you had better watch out for my sharp spears!"

Instantly, Monkey also transformed himself—into a three-headed, six-armed monkey. So ferociously did the two fight that the heavenly soldiers could not tell who was Little Immortal and who was the naughty monkey. All they could do was watch and listen to the earth-quaking, mountain-shaking roar of the combat.

The two fought from noon to evening and from evening to noon—and still there was no winner. Finally, Monkey got tired of the fighting. Instantly he changed himself back into his original monkey form. Before Little Immortal and the soldiers could catch him, he plucked a hair from his ear and turned it into a pretend monkey. Leaving his double to keep crashing his rod against Little Immortal's spear, Monkey jumped behind his enemy and gave his head a very hard smack.

"Aii-ya!" Little Immortal screamed in pain.

The soldiers burst out laughing at Monkey's clever trick.

Monkey shouted, "All right, little toy, no more of this mischief. Go back to tell the Jade Emperor that if he doesn't declare me the Monkey King, I'll pick up his palace and turn it upside down! Do you hear me?"

After transforming back into his original self, Little Immortal ran as fast as he could and was soon kneeling in front of the Jade Emperor, tears rolling down his chubby cheeks. "Father, the monkey is too powerful, I can't beat him!" He babbled on, "And there is more! Monkey also said he'd come pick up the palace and turn it over so that we're all hanging upside down like bats!"

The palace filled with noise as the officials argued about what should be done. Some wanted to tie him up; some wanted to throw him in the ocean. But no one could think of a way to catch him. Finally, the officials agreed that the best way to avoid more trouble with Monkey was to accept that he really was the Monkey King.

The Jade Emperor decided to go along with their decision until he could figure out a better way to deal with Monkey's trouble making. But that's another story.

The Monkey Wu Kong
Learns His Lesson

Now Wu Kong was back in heaven, this time as a king. He had a very simple duty—to keep an eye on the Peach Garden. He was happy because he could spend all his time walking in the garden and telling all the passersby that he was now the Monkey King.

One day the gardener showed Wu Kong some rows of peach trees. "Your Majesty, these are the most precious peaches in the whole universe. It takes nine thousand years for each of them to ripen. Anyone who eats them will live as long as heaven

and earth. So please, Your Majesty, make sure no one eats them."

"Waaahh! Is that so?" Wu Kong said, "Then I'll guard them night and day." But from that day on, instead of looking after the peaches, Wu Kong was busy snatching them from the trees and popping them into his mouth. "Aah," he sighed, munching happily away. "The Jade Emperor must know how much I love peaches, and that is why he gave me this job!"

When he had eaten so many peaches that his stomach bulged like a huge bowl, Wu Kong would transform himself into a tiny monkey, hop onto a branch, cover his belly with a leaf, and fall into a satisfied sleep. Later he would wake up and stretch, then stroll some more around the Jade Emperor's garden.

One day, the Old Queen Mother sent seven fairies and their guards to pick fresh peaches for a big party to be held at the Jade Pond. Wu Kong was thrilled to see so many pretty girls. Eyes lingering on the fairies' cheeks, which were as rosy as the ripening peaches, he asked, "Dear sisters, am I also invited to the party?"

The fairies cast him a scornful look. "Oh, we won't be inviting any monkeys to this party! Only the Buddha, Guan Yin the Goddess of Mercy, the five hundred holy ones and, of course, all the fairies are invited. Sorry," they giggled, "but we didn't hear any mention of monkeys!"

"Hah! We'll see who's invited!" Wu Kong pointed his finger at the fairies and guards, freezing them in mid-air. He somersaulted all the way to the Jade Pond. Under the trees, long tables were covered with brightly-colored silk tablecloths. Many plates of silver and gold were piled high with the tastiest foods, ready for the guests. Wu Kong plucked a few strands of hair from his head and tossed them into the air. "Wuuuff!" he blew—and the hairs turned into a dark cloud of mosquitoes.

"Buuuzzz! Buuuzzz! Buuuzzz!" As the cloud of insects swarmed around them, the fairies and the guards waved their arms, but it was no use. Within minutes, everyone had been bitten. One by one they fainted from the stings.

Immediately, Monkey jumped up to the first table and began to devour everything in sight. "Thanks, Old Queen Mother, for this wonderful meal!" he exclaimed, gulping down whole drumsticks, fish heads, bear paws, dragon liver, and phoenix marrow, till his stomach bulged like a camel's hump. By the time the fairies and guards started to wake up, all their food was gone.

"Ha, Ha, Ha, what great fun!" laughed Wu Kong as he somersaulted all the way back to his garden.

Next day, the fairies reported Wu Kong's mischief to the Jade Emperor. He yelled, "Send ten thousand soldiers to capture this smelly monkey!"

But Wu Kong still had many magic tricks up his monkey sleeve. As soon as he heard the trampling of the ten thousand soldiers' boots, he transformed himself into an army of ten thousand monkeys. The soldiers wasted all their effort in fighting pretend monkeys! Even the emperor's celestial dog could not touch a hair on Wu Kong's head. Finally, the heavenly troops realized they could not capture him and so they rushed to Buddha to beg for his help.

Suddenly, Wu Kong felt himself lifted high up into the sky. A moment later, he dropped down in front of Buddha. Looking up at the immense golden-robed figure, Monkey said, "Hey, Buddha. What's happening?"

Sitting cross-legged on a high lotus flower, Buddha looked gently at his guest and asked, his tone kind, "Monkey, why have you been causing so much trouble?"

"Because the Jade Emperor won't accept that I'm the Monkey King!"

Buddha cast him a sharp glance. "All right, so that's what you want. But let me test you first. If you can jump out of my palm, then I'll tell the Jade Emperor to accept you as a king."

"Easy!" The monkey giggled, then hopped onto Buddha's palm. "You stupid old man," he thought, "don't you know that with only one somersault, I can jump as far as eighteen thousand miles?"

Wu Kong screamed a high-pitched "Hueeeiii!" and hopped away. Within a few minutes, he had reached the edge of heaven.

"Waaahh! Even I have forgotten how good I am!" he exclaimed.

Wu Kong noticed that heaven was held up by five pillars. He had an idea—with his sharp nails, he scratched "Monkey King was here" on one of them.

Just as he was about to leave, alas, he saw Buddha towering over him like a giant wave.

"Buddha, bye-bye." Monkey waved. "I'm going home."

Buddha asked, "How? Since you're still in my palm."

"In your palm? Are you kidding, or dreaming?" Wu Kong scratched his head and laughed. "I'm at the edge of the world!"

Wu Kong looked closer and to his surprise, he saw his own handwriting "Monkey King was here," on Buddha's middle finger.

"Oh, my!" Monkey almost fainted. He realized that no matter how powerful he thought himself, or how far he traveled, the Buddha's hand could still reach him.

He knelt down before the lotus throne. "Buddha, I'm really sorry, it was wrong to cause havoc and upset everyone. Please forgive me."

"Good. I forgive you, now that you realize how wrong you've been." Buddha smiled. "Now go. But don't be such a trouble maker. You are a clever monkey—use your cleverness to help others."

"Thank you, Buddha." Monkey smiled and softly said, "It will be a tremendous challenge, but I'm sure I can find clever ways to play and have fun that will not be so annoying!"